For Ellie

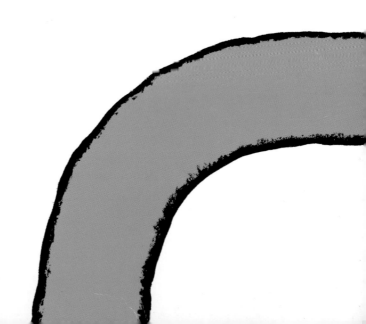

Don't Put Your Finger in the Jelly, Nelly!

by Nick Sharratt

SCHOLASTIC

Don't put your finger
in the jelly,
Nelly!

Don't put your finger
in the pie,
Guy!

The meringue-utan won't like it!

Don't put your finger
in the cheese,
Louise!

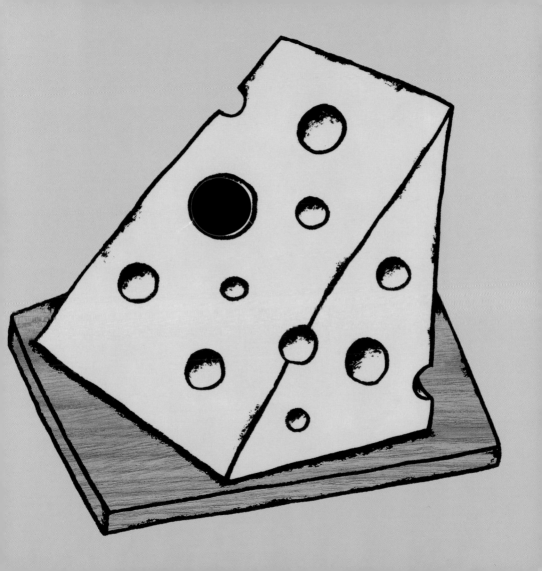

Don't put your finger
in the jam,
Sam!

It's clawberry
flavour!

Don't put your finger
in the pasta,
Jocasta!

Don't put your finger
in the shake,
Jake!

There's a
choctopus
about!

Don't put your finger
in there,
Claire!

Unless you like doughnuts, that is!

Scholastic Children's Books
Euston House, 24 Eversholt Street
London NW1 1DB
a division of Scholastic Ltd
London ~ New York ~ Toronto ~ Sydney ~ Auckland
Mexico City ~ New Delhi ~ Hong Kong

First published in hardback in the UK by Scholastic Ltd, 1993
First published in paperback in the UK by Scholastic Ltd, 1996
First published in miniature hardback in the UK by Scholastic Ltd, 2000
First published in miniature paperback in the UK by Scholastic Ltd, 2004

Photographs by Edgardo Braggio, Fotacha Ltd

Papers used by Scholastic Children's Books are made from wood grown in sustainable forests.